MY JOURNAL

By me, **KAVI SHARMA**

★ American Girl®

Scamper! Best dog ever!

Dadima & me!

Dadima is Hindi for my father's mother.

Hattie, my little elephant charm that I got in India when I was six

Sophie, me, and Pari—BFFS

WEEKLY PLANNER

BINDI COLLECTION

MY 12th BIRTHDAY!
-SEPTEMBER 30 -

Today is my BIRTHDAY! Dadima and I
baked a cookie cake because I like
cookies better than cake. I almost
forgot the flour, eek!!

COOKIE CAKE

INGREDIENTS

2 cups flour
1 teaspoon baking soda
½ teaspoon salt
1 cup shortening
¾ cup granulated sugar
¾ cup brown sugar
1 teaspoon vanilla
2 large eggs
2 cups chocolate chips

DIRECTIONS

1. In a mixing bowl, stir together the flour, baking soda, and salt. set aside.
2. In a separate larger bowl, combine the shortening, sugars, and vanilla extract. Mix until creamy.
3. Add the eggs to the sugar mixture one at a time. Mix well after adding each egg.
4. Add the flour mixture to the sugar

(CONTINUED ON BACK)

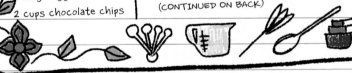

Dadima gave me the best gift EVER:
tickets for me and my friends to see
WICKED on Broadway this Sunday!!!

A cookie cake is just a giant cookie. While the cake was baking, Dadima and I danced around the kitchen with Scamper. I can't wait for my birthday dinner party tonight...

WICKED
SUNDAY AT 2:00 PM

ADMIT ONE
WELCOME
FRONT MEZ • ROW A • SEAT 108

012345 67890 0

PRINCETON

I had the best birthday party—it was a picnic with my best friends, Sophie and Pari, and Dadima, too, of course. We drove to Princeton because it's beautiful and has my favorite ice cream shop. We spread out a picnic blanket on the lawn near some big fancy buildings.

I want to go to Princeton for college. Dad went there, so he hopes I do, too. Rishi says you need smartbrainitis to go to Princeton. I wonder if my grades are good enough to get in?

OUR PICNIC WAS
THE BEST! HERE'S
WHAT WE ATE:

I snuck scamper some of my sandwich so I could save room for dessert.

sub sandwiches

samosas

cookie cake

ice cream cones

Cookies & Cream

Blue Moon

Mango

Bubblegum

Pistachio

Sophie's fave

Pari's fave

Dadima's fave (and she's picky about her mango flavors!)

Rishi's fave

I got this because it's the same color as the witch in WICKED!

Hello, Broadway! Here we are, outside the theater on Sunday afternoon. Sophie is channeling Glinda, and I'm— guess who—Elphaba!

Times Square was noisy and bustling.
As we walked to our theater, we were
surrounded by billboards, each
advertising a different show. Someday,
I'm going to see all these shows!

Then the theater doors opened, and
we went into the plush lobby, where we
checked out all the awesome WICKED
merch.

You'll never guess what was
posted at school Monday:

It's a

Revue!

Gather your **crew.**

Let's celebrate unique **you!**

Each act should be 8 to 10 minutes long
and showcase your unique talent.

Students must be in good academic
standing to participate.

I HAVE TO DO THIS!!!

But am I brave enough to do it alone?

Maybe I can persuade Sophie & Pari to do it with me . . .

Uh-oh, I didn't notice the bottom line on that poster before. I've always done pretty well in school, but 7th grade is a lot harder than 6th grade was. We have to switch classes and keep track of so many assignments. I keep forgetting to bring home my notebook. Better step up my game, so I stay in "good academic standing." (Plus, I'll need that for Princeton!)

ASSIGNMENT NOTEBOOK

BRING HOME!

After lunch was math class. We're learning about negative numbers. It's so confusing! How can two negative numbers cancel each other out?

Here's what Mrs. Roberts, my math teacher, asked us:

A and B are negative numbers.
If you multiply them, will the answer be:

1) Positive
2) Negative
3) It depends on the numbers
4) Not enough information to tell

Answer: 1) Positive (who knew?!?)

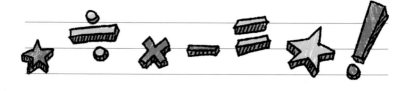

I didn't know the answer ☹. I guessed #4. So embarrassing! Pari and Sophie knew the answer. Sigh. I need to study more.

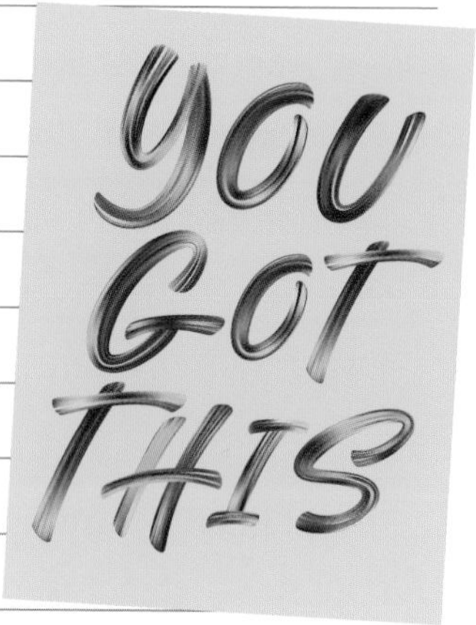

YOU GOT THIS

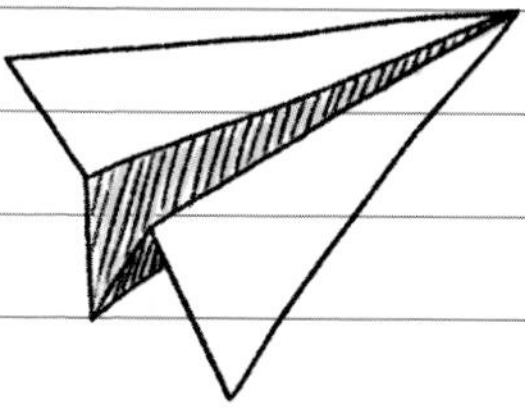

Not yet, I don't!

hELLOBLOB

Pari, Sophie, and I all take dance lessons.

Pari and I are learning a traditional dance style called Kathak. It's from North India, where my family is from.

Say it with me: KUH-thuk. It rhymes with "unstuck."

I've been taking dance lessons since I was six. I want to learn all the Indian dance styles—and the American ones, too. I've also taken Bollywood, jazz, and modern dance.

Sophie takes hip-hop.

I rushed through my homework. Now I'll
get in the musical mood before dance
class by practicing piano at the keyboard.
Can you tell I love performing? Rishi can.
He and his "medical diagnoses" are so
annoying.

Kavi has
Broadwayitis!

TUESDAY, OCTOBER 4

On the way to dance class, I asked Pari and Sophie if they would be in the revue with me. Sophie's up for it, but she wants to do a hip-hop dance.

Pari says she doesn't like the idea of performing in front of our whole school. I need to convince her it will be fun!

I told Pari, "Remember how cool those dancers were in WICKED? That could be us, dancing onstage in the revue!" But she didn't look convinced.

Even if I can find a way to convince her, WHAT KIND OF DANCE SHOULD WE DO?

The elephant is a symbol of wisdom in Hindu culture. But even Hattie didn't have an answer for me.

In fifth grade, we learned about venn diagrams. Here's mine:

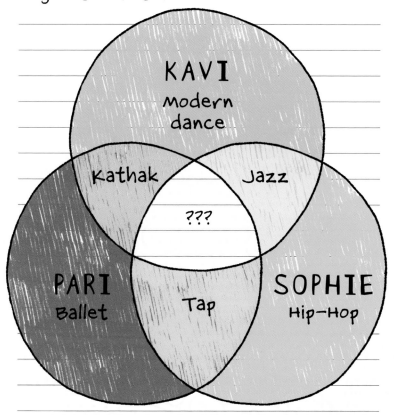

KAVI
Modern dance

Kathak

Jazz

???

PARI
Ballet

Tap

SOPHIE
Hip-Hop

We've all taken dance for years—but we've trained in different styles. I told my family we were having trouble deciding what kind of dance to do in the revue. To find out what they said, turn the page ⟶

Kathak is a beautiful traditional dance style. Of course that's what you should do. Not that hoppity hop.

I tried not to laugh when Dadima said that.

At my school, hip-hop is very popular. Hey! It's "POPular," like the song from WICKED! But Pari and I haven't taken hip-hop lessons like Sophie. Maybe Sophie's teacher could show us some hip-hop moves. But then Pari probably wouldn't want to do it at all. And Dadima would be so disappointed!

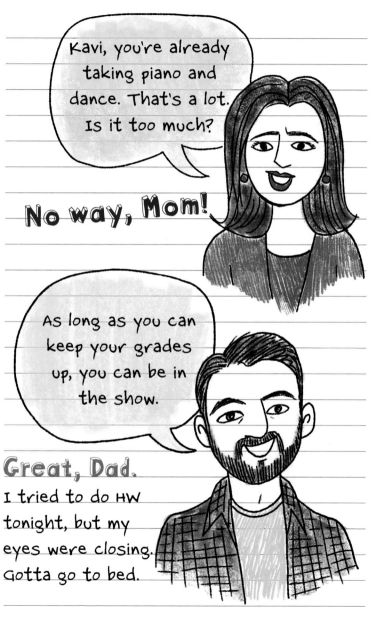

WEDNESDAY, OCTOBER 5

Last night I was exhausted and couldn't find my textbook. I keep thinking about the revue. It's hard to focus on negative numbers when you're thinking about dance numbers.

DANCE →

FLOOR

★ SING ★
DANCE
CREATE

Here's a secret about me: My brain moves FAST. It's like a TV that keeps scanning different channels!

My brain never stops on just one channel unless it's something I REALLY love. So in class, if I'm getting confused or bored, my brain switches to the looking-out-the-window channel, or the thinking-about-cute-animals channel.

It can be entertaining, but also exhausting! I can only concentrate on what the teacher is saying if I work REALLY hard to focus. Sometimes it seems like I have to work a lot harder than my friends to get my schoolwork done. It seems so easy for them.

My friends know my mind likes to wander, but they don't know how big a problem that is for me. And I haven't told them. I don't want them to think I'm weird!

THURSDAY, OCTOBER 6

Pari and Sophie got A's on the science quiz. I didn't tell them I failed it. I couldn't study for it, since I couldn't find my science notebook. ☹

Maybe I'm just not as smart as they are. But I don't want them to know that. I'm worried they might not like me as much.

I can't tell my parents either. They might say I can't be in the revue!

Kavi, I think you have Pinocchioitis. Your nose is growing!

Is not telling the truth the same thing as telling a lie?

Rishi loves the story of Pinocchio. He always asks me to read it to him.

All students participating in the revue!
Singers, dancers, musicians, jugglers,
stage crew—everyone!

Auditorium 3:15 to 4:00

Today there was a planning meeting
after school for kids in the revue.
Sophie and I are all in, but Pari says
she's still on the fence. She says
she'll think about it. I know she's shy.

But we're a trio! It just won't be the
same without her. Come on, girl! Let's
do this!

How am I going to get Pari off
the fence?

After dinner tonight,
Pari texted me:

PARI < I'm in!! 🎋

👏 💜 💜 > ME

I'M SO HAPPY! > ME

I texted Sophie right away!

Pari's in! > ME

SOPHIE < Yay! Hip-hop
till we drop!

UH-OH. HOW WILL WE DECIDE
WHAT KIND OF DANCE TO DO?

TUESDAY, OCTOBER 11

Today at lunch we argued again about Indian dance vs. hip-hop. Pari sided with me, but Sophie won't give in.

Decisions, decisions . . .

Maybe we could have a dance contest! The winner would get to choose the dance style for the revue.

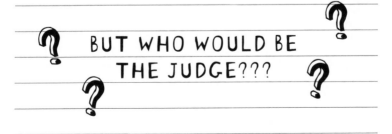

BUT WHO WOULD BE THE JUDGE???

MY ROOM IS SUCH A MESS!

It's Sunday, and this week is Diwali, so I have to clean my room. Plus, I need space so I can practice my dance routine . . . which means I have to pick up all these clothes off the floor . . . Hey, here's my missing science notebook!

OK, that's done. My floor's clean. Yay me!
Now my desk is distraction-free! And I'm
all ready for Diwali. I can't wait!

I know I should be studying, but I'm going
to practice my music for a while first.
Then I'll study. Really, I will!

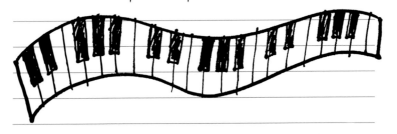

This week is Diwali! That's my favorite holiday. It's the Festival of Lights, and we celebrate it for 5 days. Diwali is about the victory of good over evil and light over darkness, but it's also about family, food, and fun!

My parents told me that I need to focus on Diwali this week and stop thinking about the revue 24/7. They like to remind me that traditions are important. ☺

HERE'S WHAT WE'RE DOING EACH DAY:

DAY 1 Clean our house. (Since I already cleaned my bedroom, I'll tackle the bathroom.)

DAY 2 Decorate our home with diyas, which are special clay lamps. So pretty!

DAY 3 Eat samosas, nimki (a crispy cumin-flavored chip), rice kheer, peanut chikki (like peanut brittle) and lots of other yummy dishes, all vegetarian.

DAY 4 Exchange gifts. Yay!

DAY 5 Visit aunties, uncles, and cousins. Eat until I'm stuffed. Then watch fireworks!

FAMILY

TUESDAY, NOVEMBER 1

Tonight after dance class, Sophie said I'm not being fair to insist on doing Kathak instead of hip-hop for the revue. But I don't see how we can do both, because they're so different—the music, the outfits, the dance steps, everything. Besides, when Pari agreed to perform, I told her we'd be doing Kathak. Still, I hate that Sophie thinks I'm unfair.

SOPHIE'S NOT HAPPY.

The truth is, I don't know hip-hop, and she doesn't know Kathak. And there isn't time for us to learn a whole new style. The revue is a week from Friday—and everyone who signed up is supposed to be practicing their acts. But we don't even HAVE an act yet!

I think Pari is just hoping we'll decide to drop out of the revue. That way she won't have to dance

IN FRONT OF THE WHOLE SCHOOL.

THURSDAY, NOVEMBER 3

Mom was cleaning out my backpack and guess what she found: my failed science quiz. She was not happy that I had hidden it from her!

Dad says if I don't improve my grade, I'll have to drop my dance class—or drop out of the revue.

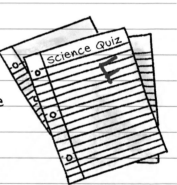

Science Quiz

F

NOOOOOOOO!

On the other hand, I guess that would
solve the problems with Sophie and Pari . . .
but I would be sooo sad.

I don't know how to fix all these problems.
My heart hurts!

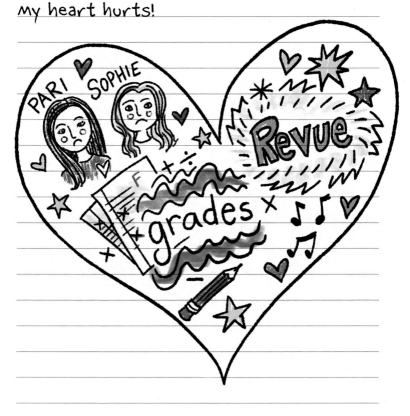

SATURDAY, NOVEMBER 5

This morning Dad invited me to his yoga class. He says yoga is a traditional practice from India that helps calm the mind.

I sure hope I don't embarrass myself! (Is that how Pari feels about doing the revue?)

If I stay home, Mom will make me do homework. So I may as well go.

Yoga turned out to be really fun. We started on all fours, arching our backs like a cat and then lowering our bellies like a cow. Then we did frog, tree, eagle, warrior, and dolphin.

The poses make you stretch and balance at the same time. It's not easy, but it's a fun challenge—kind of like learning a new dance.

Downward dog is my favorite, because it reminds me of Scamper. Plus it's a whole new way of looking at the world!

I'm a powerful warrior woman. I can do anything!

Wait, now I'm a frog. Does that mean I'm not powerful anymore?

While I concentrated on holding the poses, I couldn't think about anything else. And I learned a new way to breathe: Inhale through my nose, exhale through my mouth.

Here's a card I got to take home with me:

Asana means pose.

YOGA ASANAS

Please take proper precautions while practicing yoga.

Dad was right: yoga DID calm my mind. Afterward I felt amazingly relaxed. I think I'll start going to yoga with Dad every weekend.

On the way home, Dad told me something I never knew before: when he was a kid, he was disorganized and easily distracted, just like me. Still, Dad went to Princeton and became an architect. You have to be smart and do well in school to do that.

Dad says if I ever feel like my brain is getting all jumbled up, I can do some asanas and yoga breathing. He says it will clear my head and help me feel calm and focused. I'm going to try it.

SUNDAY, NOVEMBER 6

This afternoon Pari and Sophie came over so we could study for our science test together. I have to get a good grade on this one. I made sure to clean my room and put out snacks before they arrived.

After we'd read the chapter on cloud formations, Sophie and Pari wanted us to quiz each other.

My brain had been on the "dance channel" instead of studying my science book, so I got all the answers to their questions wrong.

"Kavi, are you reading a textbook from another planet?" Sophie asked me.

"Have Martians taken over your brain?" Pari teased.

At first I felt embarrassed and sort of hurt. But then I realized it was time to tell my friends the truth.

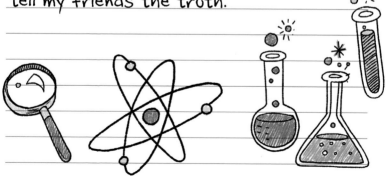

Sophie and Pari listened while I told them how my brain works. I was afraid they'd think I'm weird. But Pari just said, "I had no idea focusing was hard for you. We'll slow down."

"Wait!" said Sophie. "You love thinking about dance, right? So let's make up a dance for each cloud!"

HUH?!?

Sophie stood on tiptoes and began waving her hands in the air, saying, "I'm a cirrus cloud, wispy and way up high in the sky!"

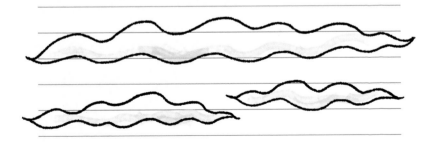

Pari jumped up. "I'm a fluffy, puffy cumulus," she laughed, bouncing on my bed like it was a trampoline. She picked up a pillow and tossed it to me. "Incoming cumulus cloud!"

So I lay on the floor and said, "Low, flat stratus cloud here!"

We all agreed this was the best science lesson ever.

But there's one thing that we still can't agree on: what kind of dance to do in the revue. Which is next week! Eeek!

Best Friends

Monday after school, Sophie, Pari, and I went to Pari's house to study together. It's our last chance to study before the test.

I love our nerdy ways!

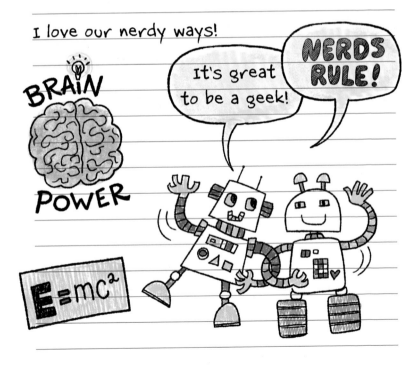

BRAIN

POWER

$E=mc^2$

It's great to be a geek!

NERDS RULE!

After a while I felt wiggly, so I got up
and did a few yoga poses. Then I did
some dance steps.

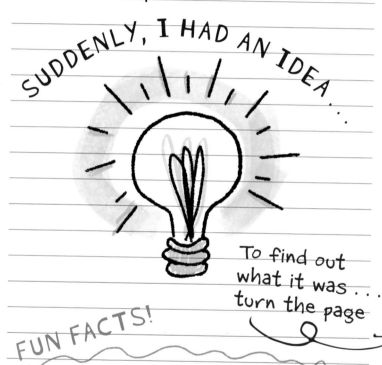

SUDDENLY, I HAD AN IDEA...

To find out
what it was...
turn the page

FUN FACTS!

Did you know that Thomas Edison, who
patented the first lightbulb, had his lab
just a few miles from my hometown of
Metuchen, New Jersey? The nearby
town of Edison is named after him.

What if our dance act starts out like a contest, with Pari and me doing Kathak and Sophie doing hip-hop. At first, we clash—our music, our moves. But then the music changes . . . and our dance becomes a Bollywood routine!

SOPHIE WAS UNCERTAIN.

Bollywood? What's that?

I told her, "Bollywood combines different dance styles, from classical Indian to jazz and hip-hop. I took Bollywood dance last year. I can teach you a Bollywood routine . . ."

KAVI
Modern
dance

Kathak

Jazz

BOLLYWOOD!

Tap

PARI
Ballet

SOPHIE
Hip-Hop

I put on some music and started moving. Pari joined in. Sophie watched for a few minutes and then started copying our moves. She's a good dancer and picked them up quickly. Then she added some moves of her own, and we copied her. Soon we had choreographed a whole dance!

We practiced it again and again until we knew it by heart. By then it was time for dinner, and we were starving.

After dinner we danced more—and studied more, too. I just hope it was enough, because the science test is tomorrow!

TUESDAY, NOVEMBER 8

Whew! That science test was hard. Still,
this time I mostly either knew the
answers, or knew how to figure them out.
I handed it in with my fingers crossed . . .

Thank goodness that's over. Now I can focus on the revue—which is good, because it's THIS SATURDAY!!! Eeek!

I've been practicing our new dance whenever I have a spare minute. (Sometimes in class, I practice in my head!)

Pari and I need to figure out our dance costumes, too. Tomorrow we're going to raid her closet for inspiration.

Here's this week's rehearsal schedule. It's intense—check it out:

Rehearsal Schedule

Tuesday 11/8	Planning meeting	Gym	3:15-4:30
Wednesday 11/9	Stage crew only	Auditorium	3:15-5:30
Thursday 11/10	Tech rehearsal	Auditorium	3:15-???
Friday 11/11	Polish your act. Get your costume ready!	At home	
Saturday 11/12	It's showtime!	Auditorium	7:00 call time 7:30 curtain up!

On Wednesday, Sophie had basketball practice, so we couldn't rehearse. Instead I went over to Pari's and tried on her older sister's Lehenga. Pari has a matching outfit in her size, and we wanted to match. It was beautiful—but too big for me. Shoot!

Then Pari's mom said Pari's sister had outgrown it, so she would alter it to fit me. She pinned it to fit, then shortened the hem and took in the waist. Now it fits perfectly! Pari said, "Thank you, Amma!" (That's what Pari calls her mother.) I thanked her, too, and gave her a hug.

Then I took a selfie of Pari and me in our matching Lehengas and sent it to Sophie.

SOPHIE 😍😍 You two look fabulous! can't wait for saturday!

On Thursday we got our tests back:

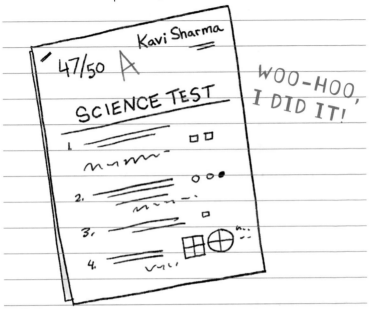

Kavi Sharma

47/50 A

SCIENCE TEST

WOO-HOO, I DID IT!

1.
2.
3.
4.

Hurray!! Mom and Dad were SO happy! No more talk about me having to drop out of dance or the revue!

What a relief—because tomorrow it's (drum roll, please)

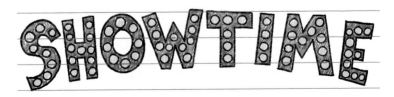

SHOWTIME

Tonight, Pari and Sophie are coming over so Mom can paint henna designs on our hands. She uses a mehndi cone, which is like a piping bag for decorating cakes, but it's filled with a paste made of henna leaves that stains the skin a red-brown color. It's an Indian tradition on special occasions. We'll show the beautiful designs during our dance. Sophie was eager to learn about henna. She felt honored when Mom said she could have it on her hands too.

SATURDAY, NOVEMBER 12

Tonight's the revue! I practice my routine over and over. Rishi keeps telling me to break a leg. Then he comes over with his stethoscope, telling me he can fix my broken leg. What a goofball!

Deep breath—in through the nose, out through the mouth. We're backstage, and the show is about to start!

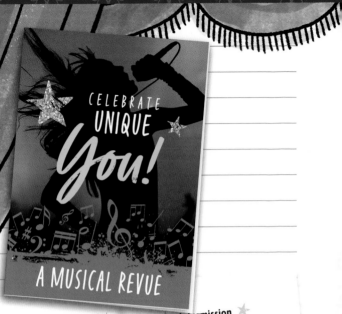

CELEBRATE UNIQUE **YOU!**

UNIQUE

You!

A MUSICAL REVUE

CELEBRATE UNIQUE YOU!
A MUSIC AND TALENT REVUE

by the students of Sheridan Middle School

★ PROGRAM ★

Welcome - Celia Tucker, director & emcee

Ballet - Jana Schulz, Mia Landry, and Aruna Sethi

Comedy - Jake Martin

Juggling - Ali Ramos

Bollywood dance - Kavi Sharma, Pari Nath, and Sophie Chandler

★ Intermission ★

Clarinet duet - Simon and Rachel Goldstein

Singing - Alaina Peterson

Tap dance - Nita Silveira and Lauren Zhou

Violin solo - Sita Gill

Grand finale - All performers!

Stage crew

Emily Martinelli, props
Kevin Van Leuwen, lighting
Neal MacPherson, sound

This is the awesome program for our revue!

Through the curtains, I can see my whole family in the front row. They look so excited to be here! I sure hope they like our dancing, even if it's not exactly what they're expecting. Our dance music is starting. That's our cue. Here we go!

AND A
5-6-7-8!

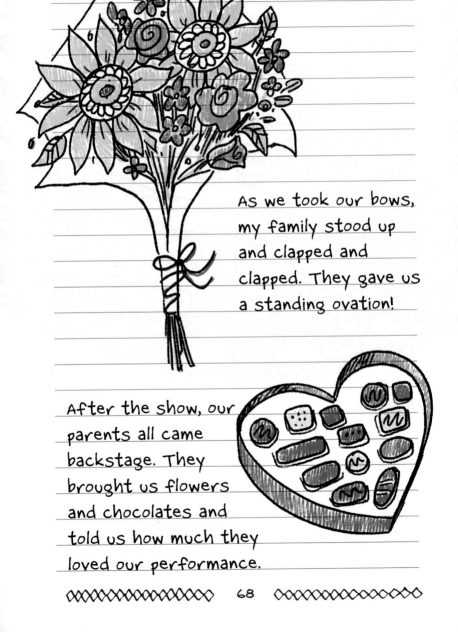

As we took our bows, my family stood up and clapped and clapped. They gave us a standing ovation!

After the show, our parents all came backstage. They brought us flowers and chocolates and told us how much they loved our performance.

Dadima hugged me and said,

You looked beautiful—just like the dancers in my favorite Bollywood movies!

Rishi announced,

Kavi, you have a serious case of Superstaritis, and I think it's permanent!

The End

☆ READER ☆ QUESTIONS

- For her birthday, Kavi's grandmother made her a cookie cake, and Kavi had a picnic with her family and her two best friends. What birthday traditions do you have in your family?

- Kavi loved seeing the Broadway musical *Wicked*. Have you ever seen a musical onstage or in a movie? If you have a favorite musical, what is it, and what do you love about it?

- Why do you think it was important to Kavi to have her friends perform in the revue with her? Have you ever persuaded a friend or friends to do something they weren't sure about? How did you convince them?

- Have you ever had a friend try to persuade you to do something you weren't sure about doing? Did you agree or not? Were you glad you did or didn't?

- If your school had a talent show or revue like Kavi's, would you want to be in it? What kind of performance would you do?

- Why do you think it was hard for Kavi to tell her friends about her trouble staying focused? What was she worried might happen? If you were Kavi, what decision would you have made?

- Kavi's favorite holiday is Diwali. What special holidays do you and your family celebrate? Do you have a favorite holiday? What do you like best about it?

Super busy with school and activities, like Kavi?

Here's how some real girls like you stay organized.
Try their tips to smooth out your day!

Every time my school binder gets full, I clean it out. I look at every paper and ask, "Do I NEED this for my learning?" If not, I recycle it. My binder is much lighter now.
—Nina

I put labels on all my drawers so I always have specific places to put everything. My room is so much cleaner and more organized!
—Bethany

I used to be in a rush in the morning. Then I found out it works really well to lay out my clothes, put my homework in my backpack, and make my lunch the night before. When I get up, I'm all ready to go.
—Makenna

I write everything I need to do on a sticky note. It's a friendly little list.
—Chloe

Because I forget EVERYTHING, I write a to-do list in a small notebook that I carry around, even at school. This makes me feel amazing! I know I can relax without worrying I forgot something.
—Maddy

I use a big whiteboard for my schedule, homework, and any other info I need to know. It makes me feel like I have all my thoughts together.
—Caitlyn

I started setting my alarm clock 10 minutes earlier, and it made my mornings go sooo much smoother.
—Gracie

I organized my whole room lately, and that made me feel REALLY fantastic!!!
—Abby

I do my homework as soon as possible because it makes my evenings more calm and relaxed.
—Flo

Get in the flow with yoga!

Yoga began in India and is now popular around the world.
When you want to feel calm and focused, try these yoga poses.

DOWNWARD DOG

Push your tailbone up to the sky.

Line up your ears with your arms.

Stretch your heels down toward the floor.

Place your hands flat on the floor.

CAT THIS POSE LOOKS LIKE A CAT STRETCHING ITS BACK!

Arch your back, rounding it and lifting it to the sky.

Move your chin toward your chest (but don't force it— it doesn't need to touch!).

EXHALE

COW

INHALE

Lift your tailbone up to the sky.

Look up, like you're about to "Moo!" to the sky.

Rest your knees on the floor.

Try switching between the cow and cat poses. Breathe in as you do the cow pose; then breathe out as you do the cat pose.

Place your hands flat on the floor underneath your shoulders.

Stretch safely! Don't force yourself into any uncomfortable positions. It's important to listen to your body and only do what you're capable of.

COBRA

Pull back your shoulders.

Look forward.

Press the tops of your feet to the floor.

Rest your thighs on the floor.

GORILLA

Lean forward and let your head hang.

It's OK if your legs aren't perfectly straight; it takes practice!

RELAX

Take two to four slow, deep breaths all the way in and all the way out while doing each pose.

Slip your hands under your toes (if you can comfortably reach) and hold this position.

DOLPHIN

Push your tailbone up to the sky.

Keep your spine straight and long.

Straighten your legs, keeping weight on your toes.

Place your arms and elbows flat on the floor.

ABOUT THE AUTHOR

Varsha Bajaj grew up in Mumbai, India—the heart of Bollywood. As a girl she loved reading and attending children's theater. When Varsha moved to Missouri for graduate school, she was lonely at first in a new country. But she found that America was familiar because of the books she had read and the movies she had seen, and soon she felt right at home. Varsha worked as a psychotherapist counseling children and families. Later she moved to Houston, Texas, where she raised her family and began writing children's books. Varsha loves Bollywood dance and Broadway musicals. Like Kavi, Varsha's daughter acted in musicals in middle school, and Varsha had a dog named Scamper!

ABOUT THE ILLUSTRATORS

Parvati Pillai is an illustrator and animator living in Finland. She is passionate about storytelling, traveling, gardening, and food. When she is not exploring the beautiful outdoors, she enjoys experimenting with new illustration styles. Parvati loves to evoke emotions through colors and hopes that her work brings a smile to people's faces. Follow Parvati on Instagram @parvatipillai.

Elisa Chavarri strives to create work that promotes inclusivity and adds happiness, humor, and beauty to this world. She hails from Lima, Peru, often drawing from her Latin culture for inspiration, and resides in Alpena, Michigan, with her husband and two young children (also great inspirations). Elisa has illustrated numerous books for children, including the Pura Belpré Honor book *Sharuko: El Arqueólogo Peruano/ Peruvian Archeologist Julio C. Tello*. She graduated with honors from the Savannah College of Art and Design, where she majored in classical animation and minored in comics.

ABOUT THE ADVISORY BOARD

Rae Jacobson, MS, is a writer, ADHD specialist, and native New Yorker. Rae's work focuses on mental health, learning differences, and women and girls with ADHD. The Senior Writer at the Child Mind Institute, Rae's writing has appeared in *Parenting, New York* magazine, and other national publications.

Masum Momaya supports artists, activists, scholars, and storytellers working for social justice—especially women, people of color, and people with disabilities—as a curator, writer, coach, and philanthropic foundation strategist. She curated a Smithsonian exhibition, *Beyond Bollywood: Indian Americans Shape the Nation,* which traveled around the United States and India.

Rina Shah is the founder and director of AUM Dance Creations and a choreographer of classical Indian dance as well as ballet, tap, jazz, and hip-hop. Born and raised in New Jersey, Rina danced competitively through college and now teaches young dancers, produces dance shows, and fields competitive dance teams at her dance schools.

Deanna Singh is Founder and Chief Change Agent of Flying Elephant, a social impact organization with a mission of shifting power to marginalized communities. An award-winning author, educator, business leader, and social justice champion, Deanna inspires others to build or break systems to create positive change.

Nina Trevens is co-founder and producing artistic director of TADA! Youth Theater, which provides kids from varied social, racial, and cultural backgrounds with original musical productions, musical theater training, and in-school residencies. Many TADA! members and alumni have careers on Broadway and in TV and film.

Allison Tyler is a counselor and social worker who provides strategies and tools for children, adolescents, and adults with ADHD to thrive. A writer and mental health advocate, she works collaboratively with schools, professionals, and the medical community to promote better understanding of ADHD.

Arusha Bargava has taken classical Indian and Bollywood dance lessons since she was five years old. Now she's thirteen and still studying Indian dance. Like Kavi, she enjoys participating in cultural and religious celebrations with her Indian American family.

Anna Degroot is fifteen and has a particular interest in understanding and raising awareness of mental health and wellness issues, especially those that impact children and school performance.

Visit **americangirl.com/play**
to discover more about Kavi's world.

Look for bestselling books from
American Girl online and in stores.

Published by American Girl Publishing

23 24 25 26 27 28 29 QP 10 9 8 7 6 5 4 3 2 1

Illustrations by Parvati Pillai, Elisa Chavarri, and Flavia Conley
Cover image by Parvati Pillai · Book design by Gretchen Becker
Brenna Vaughan pp. 72–73, Wendy Tan Shiau Wei pp. 74–75

Cataloging-in-Publication Data available from the Library of Congress

americangirl.com/service

Not all services are available in all countries.